Put Beginning Readers on the Right Track with ALL ABOARD READING™

The All Aboard Reading series is especially for beginning readers. Written by noted authors and illustrated in full color, these are books that children really and truly *want* to read—books to excite their imagination, tickle their funny bone, expand their interests, and support their feelings. With four different reading levels, All Aboard Reading lets you choose which books are most appropriate for your children and their growing abilities.

Picture Readers—for Ages 3 to 6
Picture Readers have super-simple texts, with many nouns appearing as rebus pictures. At the end of each book are 24 flash cards—on one side is the rebus picture; on the other side is the written-out word.

Level 1—for Preschool through First-Grade Children
Level 1 books have very few lines per page, very large type, easy words, lots of repetition, and pictures with visual "cues" to help children figure out the words on the page.

Level 2—for First-Grade to Third-Grade Children
Level 2 books are printed in slightly smaller type than Level 1 books. The stories are more complex, but there is still lots of repetition in the text, and many pictures. The sentences are quite simple and are broken up into short lines to make reading easier.

Level 3—for Second-Grade through Third-Grade Children
Level 3 books have considerably longer texts, harder words, and more complicated sentences.

All Aboard for happy reading!

For Eliot and Sam—E.S.

For Mom and Dad, on their 25th
Valentine's Day—T.T.S.

Library of Congress Cataloging-in-Publication Data available.

ISBN   0-448-42413-4   A B C D E F G H I J

ALL
ABOARD
READING™

Level 1
Preschool-Grade 1

Kermit's Mixed-Up Valentines

By Emily Sollinger and Tui Sutherland
Illustrated by Tom Brannon

Grosset & Dunlap • New York

It is Valentine's Day!

Kermit loves to give valentines.
He loves to get valentines, too.

Kermit goes to his mailbox.

It is full of valentines.

But—uh-oh!
There is a problem.
Not one of the cards
has a name on it!
How will Kermit know
who sent them?

Kemit
the
Frog

KER
it FR

Kermit takes the cards inside.

He sits down at the table.

Maybe the cards

will give him clues.

Kermit looks at the first
valentine.

Kermit thinks this is easy.
Only one of his friends
says "Wocka, wocka, wocka!"

This valentine must be
from Fozzie!

That wasn't so hard.
Kermit looks at the next
valentine.

Roses are red.
Violets are
blue.

Ah-ha! Kermit thinks.

So this valentine is from a rat!

It must be his friend Rizzo!
That's the only rat he knows.

This is fun,

Kermit thinks.

He turns to the next valentine.

I know a bear,
I know a frog,
a pig, a rat, a musical dog.
I'm none of these things—
I'm a...whatever!
(I'm fuzzy and blue,
and weird and clever.)
I am from outer space,
but one thing is clear:
You're all my friends,
and I'm happy I'm here.

From outer space?

Blue?

This has got to be from Gonzo!

What a great Valentine's Day!
Kermit looks at the next card.

___ibbit!
You are ___ut of this world.
The ___est uncle ever.
___ love you!
Your ___ephew

There are letters missing
from this valentine.

Ribbit!
You are **O**ut of this world.
The **B**est uncle ever.
I love you!
Your **N**ephew

Now the valentine
spells out ROBIN—
that's his nephew's name!

The next card has a message
on both sides.

A musical valentine—
it must be from Rowlf!

Kermit has only
two more cards to read.
He picks up the next one.
It looks like someone has taken
a large bite out of it.

ME LIKE FROG!
VALENTINE!
VALENTINE!
AAAAAAAAAAAAAAAAA
AAAAAAAAAAA
AAAAA!!!!!!!!!!!!!
!!!!!!!!!

Only Animal is crazy enough
to eat his own valentine!

These are all great valentines.

He looks at the very last one.

Kermie, you know we are
meant for each other
Like green berry jelly and—
yum!—peanut butter.
On the stage I'm a star;
I can't help but shine.
But always remember—
you're my valentine.

Kermit smiles.

He knows who sent this one.

Miss Piggy, of course!

Now Kermit has to hurry—
he has a lot of valentines
to give to his friends.
Will the other Muppets know
that they are from him?